This Is the Challah

By Sue Hepker

Illustrated by Amy Wummer

BEHRMAN HOUSE

www.behrmanhouse.com

This book is dedicated to my precious granddaughter,
Jillian Lara Sabsevitz. No challah could ever be sweeter!
—SH

To grandchildren, who add magic and joy to the mixture!
—AW

Design: David Neuhaus/NeuStudio
Editor: Dena Neusner

Copyright © 2012 Behrman House, Inc.
Published by Behrman House, Inc.
Springfield, New Jersey 07081
www.behrmanhouse.com

ISBN: 978-0-87441-922-1
Printed in China

Library of Congress Cataloging-in-Publication Data

Hepker, Sue.
  This is the challah / by Sue Hepker ; illustrated by Amy Wummer.
      p. cm.
  ISBN 978-0-87441-922-1
  1. Challah (Bread)--Juvenile literature. 2. Jewish cooking--Juvenile literature. I. Wummer, Amy. II. Title.
  BM657.C43H47 2012
  296.4'1--dc23
                              2012019342

This is the challah that Bubbe made.

This is the water and this is the sugar

that went in the challah that Bubbe made.

This is the yeast that frothed the water
that went in the challah that Bubbe made.

These are the eggs
that whipped the yeast

that frothed the water

that went in the challah that Bubbe made.

This is the sugar that sweetened the eggs

that whipped the yeast

that frothed the water

that went in the challah that Bubbe made.

This is the oil that softened the sugar

that sweetened the eggs

that whipped the yeast

that frothed the water

that went in the challah that Bubbe made.

This is the flour that thickened the oil

that softened the sugar

that sweetened the eggs

that whipped the yeast

that frothed the water

that went in the challah that Bubbe made.

These are the hands

that squished
the flour

that thickened the oil

that softened the sugar

that sweetened the eggs

that whipped the yeast

that frothed the water

that went in the challah that Bubbe made.

These are the braids

that were made by the hands

that squished the flour

that thickened the oil

that softened the sugar

that sweetened the eggs

that whipped the yeast

that frothed the water

that went in the challah that Bubbe made.

This is the oven that baked the braids

that were made by the hands

that squished the flour

that thickened the oil

that softened the sugar

that sweetened the eggs

that whipped the yeast

that frothed the water

that went in the challah that Bubbe made.

This is the home that is warmed by the oven

that baked the braids

that were made by the hands

that squished the flour

that thickened the oil

that softened the sugar

that sweetened the eggs

that whipped the yeast

that frothed the water

that went in the challah that Bubbe made.

This is the blessing that is said in the home

that is warmed by the oven

that baked the braids

that were made by the hands

that squished the flour

that thickened the oil

that softened the sugar

that sweetened the eggs

that whipped the yeast

that frothed the water

that went in the challah

that *we all made together.*

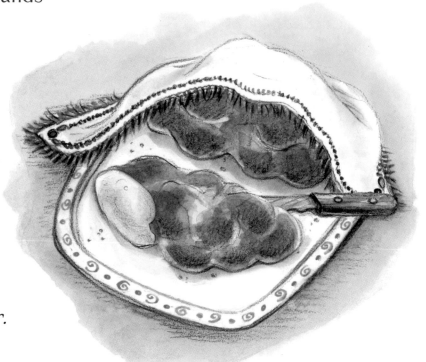

בָּרוּךְ אַתָּה יְיָ אֱלֹהֵינוּ מֶלֶךְ הָעוֹלָם, הַמוֹצִיא לֶחֶם מִן הָאָרֶץ.

Baruch Atah Adonai Eloheinu Melech ha'olam,
hamotzi lechem min ha'aretz.

Praised are You, Adonai our God, Ruler of the world,
who brings forth bread from the earth.

Bubbe's challah

Ingredients
1 tablespoon sugar
½ cup warm water
2 packets active dry yeast
4 eggs
½ cup sugar
½ tablespoon salt
½ cup oil
4 ½–5 cups flour
1 egg yolk
Raisins, sesame seeds, or poppy seeds (optional)

1. Rinse a large mixing bowl with water. Dissolve
   1 tablespoon sugar in ½ cup warm water in the bowl.

2. Sprinkle the yeast on top, and stir to dissolve. Let stand for 10 minutes. The water
   should froth. (If it doesn't, the yeast is not active, and the dough will not rise.)

3. Beat four eggs in a small bowl. Add ½ cup sugar, the salt, and the oil. Add the
   egg mixture to the yeast mixture and stir well.

4. Gradually mix in 2 cups of flour. The dough will become thick and sticky. Keep adding
   additional flour, about 2–2 ½ cups, until the dough forms a ball. Cover the dough and
   let it rest for 10 minutes.

5. Turn the dough out onto a well-floured board and knead for 10 minutes, adding flour
   if it's too sticky. Roll the dough into a ball and place in a greased bowl.

6. Cover the bowl with a cloth and let the dough rise in a warm place until doubled in
   bulk, about 1–1 ½ hours. Punch down the dough and knead it for about 10 minutes.
   Cover, and let it rise again for about 1 hour, until doubled.

7. Preheat the oven to 350°F. Divide the dough in half, then divide each half into 3 equal
   parts. Roll them into strips and braid 3 of the strips together loosely, fastening the
   ends securely. Repeat for the other 3 strips.

8. Place on a lightly greased baking sheet. Brush with beaten egg yolk and sprinkle
   with raisins, sesame seeds, or poppy seeds, if desired. Bake for 30 minutes, until
   golden brown.

   Makes 2 challahs